A Day with
Mr. Jules

A Day with Mr. Jules

=== A NOVEL ===

DIANE BROECKHOVEN

Translated from the Dutch (Belgium)
by Liedewy Hawke

DUNDURN PRESS
TORONTO

Copy Editor: Cheryl Hawley
Design: Jennifer Scott
Printer: Webcom

Library and Archives Canada Cataloguing in Publication

Broeckhoven, Diane, 1946-
    A day with Mr. Jules / Diane Broeckhoven ; translated by Liedewy Hawke

Translation of: De buitenkant van meneer Jules.
Issued also in an electronic format.
ISBN 978-1-55488-761-3

    I. Hawke, Liedewy II. Title.

PT5881.12.R56B8413 2010   839.31'364   C2010-902318-8

1   2   3   4   5   14   13   12   11   10

 Conseil des Arts du Canada   Canada Council for the Arts   Canada   ONTARIO ARTS COUNCIL CONSEIL DES ARTS DE L'ONTARIO

We acknowledge the support of the Canada Council for the Arts and the Ontario Arts Council for our publishing program. We also acknowledge the financial support of the Government of Canada through the Canada Book Fund and The Association for the Export of Canadian Books, and the Government of Ontario through the Ontario Book Publishers Tax Credit program, and the Ontario Media Development Corporation.

The translation of this book is funded by the Flemish Literature Fund (Vlaams Fonds voor de Letteren — www.flemishliterature.be).

 Flemish Literature Fund

Care has been taken to trace the ownership of copyright material used in this book. The author and the publisher welcome any information enabling them to rectify any references or credits in subsequent editions.

J. Kirk Howard, President

Printed and bound in Canada.
www.dundurn.com

Dundurn Press	Gazelle Book Services Limited	Dundurn Press
3 Church Street, Suite 500	White Cross Mills	2250 Military Road
Toronto, Ontario, Canada	High Town, Lancaster, England	Tonawanda, NY
M5E 1M2	LA1 4XS	U.S.A. 14150

Whatever we have done with our lives
makes us what we are when we die.
And everything, absolutely everything counts.

— *The Tibetan Book of Living and Dying*

THE TIMELESS HALF-HOUR between waking and getting up envelops Alice like a familiar piece of clothing. She floats in an imaginary womb, bobs towards a new day. Her body relaxes into the warm folds of the bed, her muscles and joints are weightless, her mind is a blank. Jules's smell — a whiff of evaporated alcohol, nutmeg, and old man — lies like a dark shadow behind her back. As always, he is taking care of breakfast in the kitchen, his only contribution to the housework for as long as she can remember. Every morning at the stroke of eight he starts his ritual. Alice gets up when the aroma of fresh coffee prevails over the smells of the bed and she has spent enough time counting her blessings. She struggles to her feet from her lying position and feels how the skin around her hips and thighs squeezes like an elastic stretched too tight. Her shrunken breasts huddle against her ribs. She knows that the discomforts of the first hour will vanish with brief stabs, so that by noon she will be back inside her old body. More or less.

It had snowed. Alice looked out of the window and saw the street below blazing up white. She threw her dressing gown over her shoulders to trap the warmth of the bed in the blue terry cloth. She tightened the belt around her waist and slipped her hands into the pockets. In the yellowish light of a streetlamp, Bea, the woman who lived below, was busy clearing the snow from the footpath in front of the apartment building.

"Eager beaver," Alice thought.

She stood still and listened to the alternating swishing and rasping of broom and spade, a marching brass band in the distance that never came nearer. She shivered and headed towards the coffee smell.

"It has snowed, Jules," she said to the rear of her husband's head, which stuck out above the back of the sofa. Usually, he sat waiting for her in the kitchen, at a table set according to his strict pattern. Jules gave no reply, and that made her smile. He must be staring wistfully at the snow, thinking about the old days, when there were still real winters. Icy and raw. She trudged towards him, slowed down by her stiff knees. On an impulse she let her hand rest briefly on his thin hair. Carefully putting down her feet, she walked around the leather sofa and sat down beside her husband. The fact that he deviated from his own house rules so he could take in the wintry landscape through the wall of glass softened her mood. It gave her the unexpected gift of a brief spell of freedom. She didn't need to toe the line straight away.

She slid closer to him and felt the warmth of his shoulder against hers. Just for a second, she tilted her head to one side, until the rough fabric of his vest pricked her cheek.

"It's light and dark at the same time," she said and smiled at their reflection in the large window.

Jules didn't reply. He sat perfectly still beside her, his hands on the sharp creases of his pants. In the kitchen she heard the last drops of water dripping through the coffee maker, followed by the finale of steaming and sighing. In the noisy silence that followed, reality sank in.

"Jules!"

Her voice shot from her throat, a frightened bird flapping up from the brush. She shook him, hit him, but the rigid body wouldn't budge.

"Jules!"

Another bird. A small, wary one.

He didn't react. He sluggishly yielded when she grabbed him by the shoulders, her fingers bent like claws. Jules was dead. She couldn't believe it but had to. He had died during the most blissful moment of her day, her half-hour in the womb. But first he had done his duty. He had set the table and made coffee.

It struck her as so odd that she had sat beside him and for all she knew he was alive. She had talked to him, thinking he was going to get up, walk to the kitchen with her, and sit down at the set table. The thought calmed her. Jules wouldn't really be dead until his death had penetrated her to the very bone. As yet, the truth only pulsed on the outside, in her nerve endings. It floated in through her pores like drizzle.

"It's awful for the ones who are left behind," she whispered, and the glibness of that ridiculous phrase reassured her for a moment. She laid her hand, still warm from the bed, on his, which felt cool. But not cold.

They had talked about dying, of course. They had shared their fear of degenerating into human wrecks. Jules always bristled when she said that being senile didn't strike her as catastrophic at all. It seemed a carefree existence to her. No more bothering your head with keeping things running smoothly, but nurses patiently spooning the last driblets of life into you, your little girlfriends from kindergarten, and your first, secret boyfriends, who would turn up unannounced. With that final bit in particular, she was able to get his back up. He had been her first sweetheart. He had initiated her into life and love. Even fifty years later, he didn't tolerate any jokes about so-called rivals.

"Think for a moment of those who are left behind, rather than of yourself," he would say then. "Imagine you would no longer recognize me. Or Herman, or the grandchildren."

Well, that would be the survivors' problem, wouldn't it? she thought. But she didn't express this totally self-focused opinion. It seemed so peaceful to her to vanish on the threshold of death into a bank of fog, where memories slowly faded and sounds ebbed away. She even found the dying of life in this manner romantic. The end of a French film where the colours dissolved into a pastel-coloured vista. *Fin!*

There had been moments when she had fervently longed to not recognize Jules. But he was branded into her skin. He could never become invisible to her.

To die suddenly, painlessly, without fear — that's what he would choose if he had a choice. A push in your back from a gigantic hand, no chance to brace yourself. The feeling a fly must have in the split second when the folded newspaper is raised above its doomed body. Now that was awful for those left behind. And rude, to disappear from life without any warning.

All right then, if Jules wouldn't let her drift into dementia, she opted for a beautiful, contemplative deathbed. Not too long, not too short. Pain and degrading physical details such as diapers and bluish limbs were things she repressed. She would lie in a warm nightgown between freshly ironed sheets, with a silvery grey rinse in her hair and manicured nails. She would be able to tell Jules everything she had bottled up for fifty years. That she hated him and that she loved him. That there had been times when she wanted to walk out on him and that she was glad she had stayed. That she had wanted to be free and knew she was tied to him with every fibre of her being. Things you don't say to each other in the setting of day-to-day worries. They would hold hands and forgive one another. For everything. His jaw joint would briefly move under his slackened skin, a sign for her to hold back. But in these ultimate circumstances he would control himself. He wouldn't get angry and reproach her. He would let her die in peace. Already miss her before she mustered up the strength for her last breath.

Alice was so engrossed in her fantasy that she forgot for a moment that she herself was now left behind. When this inescapable truth struck her again, her eyes filled with tears. She wiped her cheek and, with her wet hand, patted the back of Jules's hand. The chill of death was burrowing under his skin. She stood up, soaked up the white light that fell mercilessly into the room. Then she sat down on the oak coffee table, directly opposite her husband. Not sure what to do, she studied his face. His eyes were half closed, like those of a child overcome by sleep while playing. On his lips — was it her imagination, or did they have a blue tinge? — hovered the shadow of a smile. Had he felt the big hand in his back pushing him across the borderline between life and death? Only then did she notice his glasses lying on the floor. She picked them up, automatically wiped the lenses clean on a corner of her bathrobe, and slid them carefully onto Jules's nose.

He hadn't suffered, Alice knew. That reassured her. She wondered if she should close his eyes. In films, she had seen how surviving relatives pressed the eyelids shut with a delicate movement of their thumb. She got up, walked over to Jules's right, took off his glasses, and laid her hand on his face. She trembled. Last summer, she had found a little sparrow that had fallen from its nest near the apartment building. She had carried it upstairs and held it in her hand, the only conceivable place to let it die. After one last shudder it was dead, but still wrapped in warm downiness. The touch of Jules's eyelids and the nearly imperceptible caress of his lashes in the palm of her hand reawakened the little bird. She hastily withdrew her hand. She couldn't do it. The amazement on his face would disappear if she did. She sat down on the low table again. Saw the surprised, almost shy look in his eyes that made him young and vulnerable. Better to leave it this way.

When her gaze wandered down again, she saw his stocking feet on the Persian carpet. She smiled. "Oh, Jules," she said, shaking her head. "Where are your slippers? You're going to have ice-cold feet in a minute and you'll end up with a chill on your bladder."

She went to the bedroom, where the peculiar white light had filtered in, too. The window should be opened, which was really Jules's job. Now she did it herself. The

13

effort resonated through her bones and set off a chain reaction of jumbled thoughts. How would she manage? How was she going to get through the day without Jules? How would she live without him? She forced herself to think only about his leather slippers and went in search of them through the small apartment. She looked in the bathroom and, although she knew better, lifted the lid of the wicker laundry basket. Her heart was in her mouth. The totally pointless search for her dead husband's slippers prevented her from bursting out of her skin. From overflowing her banks.

They stood neatly in line under the set table, directly under his plate. This is where he must have felt the first, warning pressure from the hand in his back, Alice suspected. He must have hurried over to the sofa in his socks, before slipping over the edge of the abyss. She sat down in his chair, kicked off her own small mules, and stuck her feet into Jules's leather boats. They received her in their warm interior just as she had received Jules in the past. The emotion surging through her legs and hips into her belly stopped her for a moment from getting up. But she recovered and shuffled to the living room, where she sat down opposite him again.

"I'll put your slippers on right away, and then I'm going to have breakfast," she said to his surprised face. "For the last time, I'll drink your coffee. And I need to think, now that you don't do that for me anymore."

She leaned down and the muscles in her upper legs tightened painfully. But it had to be done.

"Come on, don't let me do all the work," she urged Jules. His left heel fitted snugly in the hollow of her right hand.

But his lifeless leg was heavy as lead. Neither his knee nor his foot would bend. Alice refused to accept defeat. She lowered herself onto her knees on the narrow strip of carpet between the table and his legs, and wrenched and wriggled until at last the two slippers were on Jules's feet. On an impulse, she slid her hands into his pant legs and took hold of Jules's legs. Her caress reached up to his bony knees. His calves breathed coolness, as if he had walked barelegged through the evening air. She lifted the hem of his pants and glanced at the bluish white shadows that gave his skin the colour of skim milk. The same colour as hers. She abruptly withdrew her hands from Jules's legs and buried them in her pockets. In the kitchen, she poured herself a cup of coffee and spread a slice of bread with apricot jam. She ate, stirred, and swallowed. She looked at the patch of bleached world outside and once again heard a marching brass band growing louder in the distance. Alternating short and long scraping by someone clearing the snow from the sidewalk. At least she wouldn't fall on her face when she went shopping later. Did she have to go shopping today? Would she ever have to go shopping again? She couldn't imagine herself alone between the supermarket shelves, without Jules stage-managing things. A nervous little laugh rose in her throat.

What was she to do? Call a doctor? Herman? He must have gone to work already. Then she would get Aimée, his wife, on the line. Alice resolutely shook her head. Herman had to find out from her that his father had died. Not in a roundabout way. Or was Aimée not a roundabout way? She got up and poured herself another cup of coffee. It helped to keep down the panic that started fluttering again. Just below her stomach this time.

She opened the refrigerator door and remembered, rather than saw, the contents. They were going to have lamb chops today, with rosemary and garlic. Jules loved them. He had put them into the supermarket cart yesterday without consulting her. Alice could never completely banish the woolly little lambs from her thoughts and usually slid her portion onto his plate.

The crisper compartment revealed the cloudlike contours of a cauliflower. The clammy taste and the shabby smell in the kitchen always reminded Alice of the grim war years. She wasn't going to have cauliflower today, and definitely not lamb chops. She tossed the meat package into the nearly empty freezer, shivering when the cold blew against her robe. Holding two greyish green fillets of sole, she hesitated, then exchanged them for a box of shrimps. Half a pound. She would eat those all by herself at lunchtime, she decided expansively. She would go to the supermarket a little later to get two big bright red tomatoes. Bulging shrimp-stuffed tomatoes, that's what she felt like. To complete the meal, she'd make fries with homemade mayonnaise. Her mother had taught her never to beat mayonnaise or bake bread when she had her period because everything was bound to go wrong then. Alice laid her hand on her belly and smiled. Her mayonnaise would turn out well and taste of the past. And Jules wouldn't spoil things by dropping a cheap jar into her shopping cart. He thought it was nonsense to stand there whisking yolks until your fingers cramped up just to save a few pennies. He explained there were salmonella bacteria in raw eggs, which could kill you. Jules knew everything. But today she chose not to worry about it.

Alice cleared the table. It didn't take long, because the cupboards, the counter, and the table were all within two steps from each other. Meanwhile, her thoughts sorted themselves out in her head. First, she would get washed and dressed, put a bit of lipstick on her dry lips, revive her sagging hairdo with the tip of her comb. While she dressed, Jules always read the newspaper. In the past, that is. Yesterday. When she came out of the bathroom, she always circled the room with her duster, following a fixed route, her gestures those of a tired conductor. In the meantime, Jules read the events worthy of mention to her. Minor news and human suffering interested her more than political intrigues and war. His collection usually involved snatched handbags, petty theft, and a murder or two. The closer the scene of the crime, the worse Alice felt about it, and the more merciless her judgement was. Do you know what they should do with someone who breaks into the place of a defenceless old woman? Yes, Jules knew. He rustled the paper as he folded it, so he wouldn't hear her torture practices.

She decided to wear the same clothes as yesterday. A brown skirt with a rusty red woollen cardigan she once knitted herself. It was a bit tight around her bosom. She was so caught up in the prospect of a perfectly ordinary day that she suddenly stood rooted to the spot in the doorway between the kitchen and the living room. It had completely slipped her mind that Jules was dead. He still sat there in exactly the same way as half an hour ago. Yet she noticed that while she ate breakfast the last trace of warmth had drained from his body. Along with the last flicker of animation. Perhaps it had registered with him too that life had escaped from all his pores.

"Relax a bit, Jules," she said. "I'll fetch the newspaper in a minute."

It was part of his morning ritual, not hers. But today all the patterns needed to be broken. Jules never went downstairs before he had washed, dressed, and shaved. They laughed together about slovenly women emerging from other apartments in faded dressing gowns to go and fetch the morning news. About men with striped pyjama legs under their raincoats, the smell of the night surrounding them like an aura. People have no manners anymore, they would say to each other.

With bent head she sniffed the smell of her own body, pulled the terry-cloth tie of her dressing gown firmly around her waist and sat down in front of Jules on the coffee table. She would have sworn he smiled.

"I'll put on my coat over my nightclothes and listen first for rumbling in the elevator shaft," she reassured him.

No one was going to notice that she, too, had lost her manners. She wouldn't give anyone a chance to ask how Mr. Jules was.

His presumed smile took on a slightly worried twist. Did he arch his eyebrows for a fraction of a second? Or did it only look like that? She dismissed the thought of the supermarket. She would just imagine those tomatoes this afternoon. She shouldn't go and walk around the store by herself. Everyone would ask after Jules. What was she to say then? That he was sitting, dead, on the sofa at home? He wasn't dead as long as she told no one. He was alive for as long as she wanted him to be. She still had so much to tell him. It would all surely come to her as the day progressed. Everyone should leave her alone today.

She resolutely got up and, on an impulse, stroked his cheek. She froze. He was ice-cold, his skin had turned to marble. Life seemed to be draining away from her too. She dropped down on the sofa beside him and pressed her face against the rough tweed of his shoulder. A dog begging for warmth. An unmistakable chill had taken possession of his whole body and penetrated his clothes. His male smell had also vanished, and she missed that even more than his physical warmth. Soap, skin, coffee, familiar pet — it was gone. He sat there like a skillfully executed copy of Jules in Madame Tussaud's wax museum. Alice cried. Her tears dripped into his shoulder pads and fell on his yellowish right hand. When she stood up, she could feel his body briefly leaning towards her and then righting itself again.

She had better forget about the newspaper and lie down beside Jules, her head in his lap. She should start making phone calls. But she checked herself. If doctors, neighbours, and undertakers began to take charge of her husband, he would be lost to her in an hour. For ever. They would carry him out of the apartment within the hour. In a coffin, which they'd have her point out in one of those albums. She couldn't let that happen, could she?

She hurried to the side room and took a plaid blanket out of the closet. In a flash, she spotted the chessboard on the small antique table, with all the pieces at the ready for a game.

David, she thought with a start. She had forgotten all about David. At ten sharp he'd be at the door for his chess game with Jules.

The blanket. The newspaper. The time. David. The four subjects tumbled around in her head and gave her wings. She flew to the kitchen, saw on the clock that it was not yet a quarter to nine. The plaid blanket had once lain on the backseat of their first car, a stately Fiat 1400 with plump cheeks and a high back. She put it over Jules's knees.

"There you are, dear," she said softly. "Otherwise you'll get much too cold."

Now that she no longer saw his bluish white hands, with the network of stiffened veins beneath the skin, he looked less dead than he was. Next, she grabbed her navy blue raincoat from a coat hook in the hallway and slipped it on over her dressing gown. In the mirror, she saw three layers of fabric bunching up around her knees. I look a fright, she thought, remembering with a smile an expression of her youth. Girls nowadays didn't say that anymore. She poked her head tentatively into the little hallway, where another apartment opened out on as well. A young working couple lived there. They would surely be stuck in some traffic jam by now. She pressed the worn-down elevator button, into which her finger fitted perfectly, and heard the mechanical sighing and groaning starting up. In the little cage, she whizzed down six floors. She clutched the bunch of keys in her coat pocket as if it were a life buoy.

The lobby, looking glaringly bright because of the snow, was deserted. The marble floor showed a path of wet footprints. Alice glanced down at her own slipper-clad feet, at her thin, bluish ankles. She would die if anyone saw her like this. The newspaper stuck out of

21

the mailbox, she didn't even have to open the little door. That saved time. Luckily, the elevator had waited for her, and within seconds Alice was back at her front door.

She turned the key in the lock with shaking fingers and entered her own domain. Breathless and numb with cold.

"I'm going to take a bath, Jules, whether it's Wednesday or not. I am frozen," she said while she laid the newspaper on his lap.

She poured a splash of lavender oil on the tub's white porcelain, turned the hot-water tap wide open, and groped in a drawer for her plastic shower cap. Wet hair at the nape of her neck upset her and ruined the collar of her cardigan. She shoved her curls under the elastic and undressed in the stiflingly hot room. Before sliding into the water, she stepped into the hallway naked, with that ridiculous bonnet on her head.

"In the bath I'll think of what to do about David," she called out to the back of Jules's motionless head. "Perhaps I can phone Bea and tell her you had to go out unexpectedly. Or that you have a touch of flu. But then she is bound to come and babble on about herbal tea or steam baths. Don't worry. I'll come up with something. We've got another hour."

A Day with Mr. Jules

What for an ordinary person would be no more than a habit that had begun purely by chance and could be broken at any moment, was for David, the boy downstairs, something to hold onto during the idle days of his school holiday. His daily game of chess with Mr. Jules was an island in time, a black-and-white checkered refuge. They always began at the beginning, each in turn making the first move. At half past ten, David swept all the pieces from the board with a clatter, regardless of what point they had reached. Only once had they managed to finish a game within the allowed half-hour. David was the winner, but that left him totally cold. It wasn't the game or winning that counted for him, but the safety of a constantly repeated habit. The boy had the face of an angel, contrasting oddly with his lanky, rangy body, which moved as though it ran on batteries. He rarely spoke. He observed, soaked up impressions and moods, smiled and kept silent. Life unfolded like a play he carefully directed himself. He lived three floors down in the same apartment building, with his mother, Bea. Alice had never seen a father or any other family member. And it wasn't like David to answer questions about facts that occurred outside his field of vision.

A year ago, shortly before noon, they had met him in the elevator. The boy's reluctant gaze first wandered from her to Jules and then fixed on a point above their heads. There was no reaction when Jules asked him if he was on holiday. They were part of the air he breathed, nothing more. Jules's opinion about today's ill-mannered children was on the tip of his tongue. Alice knew it would roll off as soon as they shut their own door behind them. As for her, she was moved by the boy. She couldn't quite tell how old he was. His upper lip already showed the shadow of a man, but the sturdy calves under the wide pant legs were those of a child. He reminded her of Marcellino *pane e vino*, the boy in the Italian movie that had moved her to tears as a child. Jules snorted.

"David is autistic," Bea said, used to recognizing the disapproval of adults by their sighs. "And he's a bit angry today. Otherwise he would certainly have said that he is on fall break. Isn't that so, David?"

"And why are you angry?" Alice had asked. Asked him, not his mother, because she wasn't quite sure what autistic was.

He had looked hard at her. Inhaled her like air. But he didn't reply.

"He has just learned to play chess at school," Bea explained. "He is obsessed by it, but I don't know how to play, so …"

"I wouldn't mind playing a game of chess with you. I'm sure you'll win because I haven't played for ages. Why don't you come over this afternoon, around three?" Jules offered.

Alice felt a pang of love for her husband at that moment. A smile briefly lit up David's eyes.

"Tomorrow, at ten," he said softly. It was a tone that admitted no contradiction.

Bea laughed. "He likes to stick to his routine. At school, chess is at ten o'clock."

And that's how it began. The following morning at the stroke of ten, David went up three floors with his mother and was left in the identically constructed apartment. In the presence of the boy, Jules became autistic too. They didn't say a word, just sat there across from each other in oppressive silence, taking turns moving a chessman. Ceremonies such as offering a cookie or a glass of chocolate milk were not in order. David came to play chess. Not to eat or drink.

Since that first time, he had come every day of his holidays at ten sharp. Alone — that's what he insisted on. His mother put him in the elevator on the third floor, and on the sixth he got off and rang their doorbell.

"Hello, Mr. Jules. Hello Mrs. Alice," David said. At exactly half past ten the game was broken off.

The bathwater was like candlelight. It softened the contours of Alice's old body and smoothed out the folds in her loose skin. Never again would Jules lay his hand on her belly, never again say that her skin was like that of an overripe peach. It used to be tight and glossy like that of an apple. She purposefully stepped out of the water, rubbed herself dry with a towel that was still damp from

25

Jules. The cells of his body intermingled with hers. While she spread the towel over the radiator, her thoughts jumped a few seconds ahead of the present. Her mind opened like a flower for the newspaper reports Jules was about to read to her. Afterwards, they would discuss what they were going to have for dinner. And then shop.

She had to swallow her irritation when the back of Jules's head reappeared in her field of vision. How could she have forgotten again that he was no longer part of this world? When she sat beside him, she grew painfully aware of her own warmth. She noticed once more that his profile seemed to be carved out of marble. The groove embedded in his upper lip, the folds in his neck, the razor-sharp scores running from his nostrils to his mouth corners. His skin had turned to stone. She gingerly stroked his cheek with her finger, touched the age spots on his temple. Jules had stiffened into a sculpture, a reproduction of himself.

"Jules! Can you still hear me?" she asked urgently, feeling the curve of his outer ear. The lobe, once softness incarnate, was as hard as a polished pebble.

She wanted to pull the plaid blanket over her own knees when the telephone rang. Her stomach tightened.

It was Bea.

"Mrs. Alice, I have a big problem." Her voice sounded as if someone were chasing her. Panicky and rushed. "My mother fell in the snow this morning and was taken to hospital. She has probably broken her hip. I have to go to see her, but David gets dreadfully upset in unexpected situations. And he doesn't want to miss his chess game. Can he come half an hour earlier?"

Alice was struck dumb. She had let all thoughts of David drain away with the bath water. What should she say? That it wasn't convenient because Mr. Jules was sitting dead on the sofa? Bea was an energetic woman, always willing to do someone a good turn. She wouldn't hesitate to set the machinery in motion. The man with the album full of coffins would appear. Herman and his wife would be ensconced in her chairs within half an hour, pour the last drops of Jules's coffee into the sink, and make a fresh pot to recover from the shock. They would comfort her before she had comforted herself. Alice couldn't cope with that. Not yet. First, she needed to say goodbye to Jules, before she could let him go. She wanted to have a private talk with him, tell him everything he still needed to know.

"Actually, I have a problem too."

Wrapped in warm breath, the words tumbled out of her mouth. "You see, my husband isn't feeling very well. A touch of the flu, I think."

She heard Bea sigh three floors down. She even thought she detected a sob.

"Oh well, send the poor boy over anyway. We have to help one another in times of trouble, don't we?" Alice decided on the spur of the moment. "If need be, I'll play a game of chess with him."

She couldn't tell a rook from a pawn, but she would think of something. She yearned for an ordinary day full of fixed points, including David. It would help her to stay calm and accept reality. Every hour a measured dose.

"How kind of you, Mrs. Alice," sounded Bea's voice. "But it won't be easy. It isn't David's time yet, and he won't like having another chess partner. But this is an emergency. Can I send him up right now?"

She couldn't go back on her word.

"Just put him in the elevator. I'll be waiting for him," she said.

Her hand shook when she replaced the receiver. Jules made no comment.

"I'm sure David likes checkers too," she thought out loud, hoping for Jules's approval. But it remained quiet in the room. Deathly quiet, and white.

She carefully closed the living-room door behind her and stationed herself on the landing. Perhaps Bea would accompany her son in these unusual circumstances. She already heard the humming and squeaking in the bowels of the building. But David stepped out of the elevator alone. When he saw her, his eyes darkened a shade. He briefly clenched his hands into fists. Then his fingers escaped from their own grip and played a fierce *étude* in the air.

"Come on in, David," Alice said, ignoring his fluttering hands. "Mr. Jules is a bit under the weather, but I am going to play a game of checkers with you. I just have to go and look for the pieces."

She steered him into the small side room, saw how he brushed some imaginary dust from the chair seat, how he sat down ramrod straight in front of the chessboard. He didn't talk. So she chattered away. Her words flitted about the room like butterflies. In the meantime she searched in the closet for the cigar box with the painting of Elisabeth Bas on the cover, in which the sixty-four checker pieces had been kept for many years.

'Did your grandma slip in the snow?" she babbled. "Then she must have gone out early this morning."

She placed three identical wooden boxes on the table. In the first, she found playing cards and an Old Maid game. In the second, small envelopes with foreign coins. In the third, finally, the white and black discs.

"Aha, there they are. Now we'll hunt up the cardboard checkerboard, so we won't need to disturb the chess pieces. Mr. Jules had already set them out last night. You know there's a checkerboard on the back of the chessboard, don't you?"

She sympathized with David, who was silent as the grave. She understood his longing for fixed patterns in fixed places, caught in the iron grip of time. A person could ward off fate by playing the right game at exactly the right moment. She reached for the box, patched up with yellowed Scotch tape, in which she suspected to find the checkerboard, folded in two, with the Sorry game on the back. In the coloured circles, years of exasperation were clustered together. The tears of Herman, who was a poor loser and revealed this in moist explosions, had congealed between the lines.

Under the checkerboard, she suddenly spotted the magazine. She held it in her hands, caught the light in the glossy, black cover. She could still see the impressions of the letters. Time hadn't erased them. At a glance she recognized Jules's handwriting in the deep grooves. The black surface sucked her down. She disappeared underwater. She swam in time.

David, who still sat ramrod straight behind the chessboard with cautiously flitting fingers, had vanished from her mind.

Until his despair about all that was different today was released in a shrill cry.

"I don't want to play checkers!" he shrieked, and swept the checkerboard and cigar box from the table. The discs rolled slowly in every direction and spun to a stop. David sucked his lungs full of air and in the same breath blurted out three more sentences. Staccato.

"I don't want snow and I don't want to play checkers at half past nine and I don't want Mrs. Alice."

He bowed his head. His shoulders dropped. He briefly glanced at her like Marcellino *pane e vino*. Then he looked down again and she saw tears clinging to his dark eyelashes.

"I want to play chess with Mr. Jules. At ten o'clock," he whined.

"Mr. Jules is a bit under the weather," Alice said firmly.

"Is he in bed?" David asked after a short pause during which he had formulated his question.

"No, he is sitting on the sofa in the living room," Alice answered. "He is looking out at the snow."

David got up and kept his leaping hands under control by clenching them under his armpits.

"Come," he said to Alice.

She didn't protest. She might as well take the boy to the living room so he could see for himself that Mr. Jules was incapable of playing chess today. Under the weather, stiff, unworldly, or moulded in wax: perhaps to David it was one and the same thing.

When they stood by the sofa together, close to each other but carefully avoiding touching one another, David studied the scene. Then he broke away from Alice's shadow and went up to Jules. He laid his hand on the petrified forehead and blew gently against the thin hair. It stirred almost imperceptibly in the warm puff of air and made Jules a little bit alive again. Alice's hand moved all by itself to the spot where she heard her heart pumping away. It was involuntary. David looked just like an angel, the way he stood there leaning over her husband. A being from another planet who had come to collect Jules, and breathed a whiff of new life into him for the final journey.

"Mr. Jules isn't under the weather. Mr. Jules is dead," David said.

"Well, yes," Alice admitted. "I am quite aware of that."

With solemn steps, too grave for a child, he strode out of the room. Alice scurried after him. She saw how he sat down at the chessboard, ran his eyes over the pieces. He painstakingly moved the white pawn in front of the king two squares forward. Next, he put his index finger on the black pawn and moved it. He took the place of Jules himself, and Alice was almost sorry that her husband turned out to be so easy to replace. David became totally absorbed in the game, in his strategy of thinking ahead and yet staying in the here and now. With a determined tap he alternately moved a white and a black chessman. Apart from Jules's empty chair, everything was identical to yesterday and the day before. They were even back on schedule. It was ten past ten.

Alice stood at the window and leafed through the photo magazine. The memories pounced on her like a swarm of flying ants. They loomed out of nowhere. Somewhere in the middle, she found the letter she once wrote to Olga but never sent off. More than thirty years later, she was grateful for that. I know you are sleeping with him, although he maintains emphatically that all you do is talk, she read. Her eyes raced over the lines. She didn't dare let the words sink in. If only you had stayed where you belong, behind the Iron Curtain ... When that sentence leapt out at her, her hand automatically crumpled the paper into a ball, which she slipped, crackling, inside the pocket of her cardigan.

David was so engrossed in his chess game, he didn't even notice that Alice left him on his own. The newspaper had slid down from Jules's knees, and this alarmed her. Had he moved? Was his body beginning to swell, or deflate, rather, so that it shifted slightly? She put the photo magazine in front of him on the coffee table.

"Later, when David has gone home, I'll tell you how I found out," she said, and there was excitement in her voice. "There's no such thing as the perfect murder or the perfect adultery."

On the kitchen clock it was nearly half past ten. She had no idea how much longer David would stay, and in order to have something practical to do she started the lunch preparations. She peeled two robust potatoes and put them in a small pan on the stove. Then she let the last egg she found in the refrigerator slide from a spoon into the same water. The shrimps had thawed. Alice shook them into a bowl and topped them with a spoonful of mayonnaise. She had lost all inclination to bustle about with oil and vinegar, and, besides, she realized she had used up her last egg. She had visions of holidays at the seaside, plates with fried sole, a handful of lettuce and a small mound of fries. And a glass of wine. She was going to have white wine this afternoon, though Sunday was a long way off.

A bottle of Sauternes lay in the refrigerator. But how would she manage to open it, with her arthritic hands and a reluctantly flapping corkscrew? Could she ask David perhaps? She set the bottle on the table, saw a moist film appearing on the glass right away. While the potatoes were cooking, she glanced through the paper. Jules was only one of the many dead today. She impatiently refolded the sections, relieved that Jules didn't see this anymore. According to him, a newspaper should look exactly the same before and after it has been read. He had told her hundreds of times. Ignorant of three quarters of the world news, she flung it into a box full of waste paper.

She fished the hard-boiled egg out of the pan and went to sit beside Jules again. Suddenly, she felt exhausted.

"Why didn't you die in bed?" she asked. "Then we could have taken a nap under the covers together."

She shivered when she leaned against his shoulder and felt the chill of his body creeping into hers. She closed her eyes for a moment, was startled by David who, without warning, stood before her.

"Mr. Jules, you won," he said. "Tomorrow you get to make the first move."

"David, can you open a bottle of wine?" Alice asked.

She led the way to the tiny kitchen and rummaged around in a drawer until she found the corkscrew.

"A corkscrew is a lever," David said, and drove the spiral forcefully into the cork.

In the meantime, Alice prodded the potatoes. She would leave them to cool, and fry them this afternoon, sprinkled with mixed herbs, which Jules loathed. Food should simply slide over your tongue and down your throat, in his opinion. It shouldn't contain any bones, stalks, veins, or pips.

"Nectar from heaven," David said as he pushed the opened bottle across the table towards her.

It was the first time she heard him say something that wasn't functional.

"Does your mom always say that when she drinks wine?" Alice asked, yearning for some conversation.

"Yes," David said.

The dialogue was over.

There was nothing left for them but to wait until Bea came home and reclaimed her silent son. David retired to the safe fortress of the little side room. From the doorway, Alice saw how he stowed the chessmen in the box and then took them out again one by one. He felt them, set them back with precise gestures in the spots where they belonged. Ready for a new game. Perhaps she should make him a present of the chessboard, as a souvenir of his quiet holiday meetings with Mr. Jules.

For the umpteenth time, Alice covered the distance between the side room and Jules. What she really wanted to do was lie down, lay her head on his marble thigh, close her eyes, and forget everything. But if Bea called, she wouldn't be able to instantly jump to her feet with her stiff knees.

From the leather armchair she had a totally different view of her husband. His profile seemed sterner, sharper. Alice waited, her hands in her lap. Under her own skin, she felt life rustling and tingling, in spite of the many layers of fabric.

The time dragged heavily. The world turned at half speed. And shot out of its orbit when the doorbell rang.

"My God," Alice muttered. "What should I do now?"

Before God could answer, she was already at the front door. She pressed her eye against the peephole. Bea stood in the hall. Snowflakes, disintegrating into dew, glistened on her shoulders.

"There's your mother, David," Alice called out, while simultaneously pulling the living-room door hermetically shut.

The cold of outdoors clung to Bea and made Alice shiver. It was a living, moving kind of cold, mixed with warm breath and a faint smell of women's sweat. Unlike the massive chill that had sunk its teeth into Jules. David already stood beside her. His hands fluttered and his eyelashes trembled. Something was wrong, Alice knew.

"My mother isn't doing well. She'll be operated on this afternoon. I may have to drop in on her again this evening. She hit her head on the curb when she fell. I have a bad feeling about it …"

The words spurted from Bea's lips. David tensed the back of his neck, suddenly had a triple chin and briefly sucked in his breath. It looked like the buildup to a shriek. But no sound came out. Only his hands spoke, kneading in space.

"And your husband? Has he recovered? David hasn't been troublesome, has he?" Bea asked while she intertwined her fingers with those of her son.

Alice took hold of one of the boy's hands and one of his mother's, and thereby calmed the wriggling snake pit.

"Not at all. He has been a very good boy, actually," she said. She looked David straight in the eye, felt his fingers in her left hand relaxing.

"Mr. Jules won," he said to his mother.

"That's nice. I'm glad he isn't too ill to think, then."

Bea withdrew her hand.

"Come, David. We're going. Be polite now and say thank you. Have you said goodbye to Mr. Jules?" she added for form's sake. She knew that her son didn't go in for formalities.

"Is Mr. Jules in bed? Does he have a fever?" she asked.

Drops trickled from her dark hair when she turned her head abruptly towards Alice.

"No," Alice replied. "He is sitting on the sofa in the living room. I put a blanket over his knees. I'm pampering him a bit today."

David looked at her. His face was blank, unreadable, but she knew that he was her ally.

"I want to take the elevator on my own," he told his mother. And to make doubly sure, he repeated it. Loudly and clearly.

"All right. I'm on my way then. Thanks, Mrs. Alice, and I hope your husband will be better soon."

Bea whizzed down three floors to meet her son.

In the minute that David waited by Alice's side for the elevator to return, he said with undisguised triumph: "Mr. Jules won."

"You can say that again," Alice agreed.

"I'm dying for something to eat, Jules," she said, and she chuckled at the ambiguity of her words. In the kitchen, she felt the potatoes between her thumb and index finger to check if they had cooled. But she had no desire any-more to fry them in a big pat of butter. She cut them, cold, into slices, a pale rock formation next to the shrimps. She settled herself down in the leather armchair with the plate on her lap and bolted everything down in a couple of minutes.

"Delicious," she smacked, the corners of her mouth clogged with mayonnaise. She had a need to get Jules's back up, to behave like a barbarian. Hadn't she sat primly at the table all her married life, eaten with knife and fork and dabbed her chin and lips with a napkin — paper on weekdays, linen on Sundays and public holidays?

She had forgotten the wine. After her meal, which hadn't lasted more than five minutes, she filled two gold-rimmed glasses and put one down in front of Jules.

"Cheers, Jules," she said as she raised her glass in his direction. "Here's to all we've been through together."

She drained the glass to the last drop, as though it contained water, exchanged it with his, and gulped that down, too. Then she began to cry uncontrollably.

"Oh Jules," she wailed. "Why are you doing this to me? This isn't what we'd agreed on, is it?"

She jerked the plaid cover off his knees and snuggled down against him. She tried to trap a bit of warmth by tucking the blanket in tightly on her side, but after a minute or two she had become almost as cold as he was.

"You'd think it was contagious," she shivered.

The wine had made her legs feel leaden. She ought to take a nap and get warm again before sitting down beside him with the photo magazine. In the bathroom, she ran the tap until the water was hot and steamy, and she filled a hot-water bottle. Then she lay down on the sofa, with a cushion between the back of her head and Jules's icy thighs. The rubber bottle, out of which she had carefully squeezed the surplus of air, lay like a second belly on top of hers. Flab on flab. Sleep overcame her. She dreamt she was pushing a cupboard through the room. The unwieldy legs groaned across the parquet floor. Jules bawled her out and furiously waved his arms. When she woke up and closed her bone-dry mouth, the pushing stopped at once. And Jules was still dead.

From her lying position, she gazed at his double chin. The fleshy layers looked frozen, and formed one whole with the collar of his blue shirt. Carved out of stone and painted in afterwards. The hair sticking out of his nostrils like two tiny, fine paintbrushes moved her.

"I knew it, Jules," she said, coming straight to the point. She lay as still as she could, so she wouldn't stir up the warmth that enfolded her. "I knew there was something going on between you and Olga, perhaps even before you knew it yourself. A woman can see that coming. She knows it, tastes it, smells it. An affair sticks to a man, to his skin and his clothes, to his words and his indifferent silences. But you didn't know that I knew. This didn't change when we went on holiday together. The two of us in Italy, where we would take all the time in the world for each other and wanted to make a fresh start after all my distrust and suspicions. You did your best — I have to say that much for you. You did things you normally never bothered with, and then I am not talking about the siestas in the wide bed while outside the Vespas sputtered past. We rediscovered each other. I believed you when you told me you had been in love with her, but that one can suppress love and longing. Just like hunger, just like thirst. And yet I knew you were lying too, although they were only tiny, trivial lies. We bought ten postcards and twelve stamps. *Francobolli*. I knew you were cheating on me with those two extra stamps. That you wrote to her in stolen moments. At the antique table near the window, while I sat in the claw-footed tub, basking in the after-glow of our lovemaking. Or in an outdoor café, when you wanted to roam around the town by yourself for a while to buy a souvenir for me. A silk scarf with slender, delicate trees in a pastel green landscape..I still have it. I'll go and look for it in a moment. Perhaps I'll wear it at your funeral. Silk is appropriate for any occasion."

Some of her words broke the silence. Others formed inside her mouth and remained unspoken. What did it matter? She knew Jules could understand what she meant. She paused and looked up, as if she expected him to protest.

"A nice touch of colour to my grey winter coat," she reassured him. "I don't have to be all in black, do I? I will wear my Italian scarf, and that's final."

Your clothes are your concern, he had snapped out year after year, whenever she asked his approval about a skirt length, a fabric, a colour. But when she coquettishly came to show him some new purchase, or an outmoded dress she had infused with new life by adding a brooch or a new collar, it was always wrong. Too yellow. Too young looking. Too heavy. Too provocative. Never having to ask for his opinion anymore would take some getting used to. From now on, she would do as she pleased. The thought made her eyes fill with tears again.

"I'm getting up, Jules," she continued, tossing the blanket aside and straightening up. "Now I will finally show you the evidence."

She picked up the magazine and ran her palm over the glossy black surface. For a few seconds her anger flared up violently, like a heartburn attack. She brandished the rolled-up magazine near Jules's face, which made his hair stir gently again. This calmed her at once.

"I read the imprint of your letter to Olga," she said.

For thirty years, it had been on the back of her tongue, and now she had said it.

"Remember you bought a new camera for our trip?" she asked.

A Day with Mr. Jules

Their old Geva Box had given up the ghost during the Christmas holidays of that eventful year. They had crowded into lots of family snapshots, tightly squeezed together, half-hidden behind the tinsel. The lean years were over: Jules had bought a Minolta.

"This magazine came with it," Alice said.

She felt her own clammy fingerprints on the black, glazed paper. "I can still see it lying on the writing table by the window in our Italian hotel room, Jules," she went on. "And then you were in the bathroom. Night was falling and I heard the hum of your electric razor. I had already put on my evening gown. Too revealing, but I don't think you minded then. I switched on the table lamp, and in the yellowish light that fell on the black, I saw letter imprints. Your handwriting — I'd be able to pick it out of thousands. When I caught the light on the paper in just the right way, I could read entire passages. That's how hard you had pressed. Olga, Olga, Olga. I spotted her name at least three times in a single glance. The capital letter *O*, open and obscene, jumped off the paper. I read that you would go on holiday with her, too. It would be a thrill. And no one would know. How much you loved her! More than you had ever loved anyone. It was written there. I only needed to make the page dance under the lamp to see for myself how you cheated on me.

"We didn't go to the opera that night. Even before you came out of the bathroom in your black suit, I was

43

burning with fever. In your smell of bubble bath and aftershave, I sat in front of the toilet bowl in my revealing evening gown and retched. A little later, when I lay on the bed, sweat beaded on my upper lip and between the roots of my hair. With your snow white shirt as a beacon of light around you, you ushered in a doctor who enforced his Italian monologue with a brisk shot in my buttock. I slept one night and one day. I needed twenty-four hours to let the humiliation and the heartache drain away down to my deepest layers. I didn't want to lose you, Jules. You were my other half. I would have gone against my nature if I had let you go then."

"We never knew what that doctor said. And you maintained it was from the olive oil. In those days, that could still be used as an alibi for every holiday ailment."

Alice shrugged.

"Olive oil," she sneered.

She switched on the lamp and held the magazine under the light. Her heart pounded. Jules's passion had survived wonderfully well all those years. She put her glasses on the tip of her nose, narrowed her eyes, and amid the jumble of the letters she saw the *O*'s of Olga lighten into perfect circles again. She could still read the sentence in which he promised to go on holiday with her. Or was it etched in her memory rather than in the black paper?

"But you didn't go on holiday with her," she said maliciously. "*I* saw to that."

A Day with Mr. Jules

After their stay in Tuscany, spying on Jules, sniffing at him, catching him became a full-time job. She thought she heard a suspicious undertone in every telephone conversation. Under her anxious gaze, a greying hair on his shoulder became pitch-black. In bed, she would turn away from his body almost in disgust because she was sure he was no longer hers alone. But in the deepest, darkest hour of the night, yearning for the oblivion of sleep, envious of his regular breathing, she suddenly longed to possess him. She seduced and mounted him. She forced him to love her and stir up her pain. He never turned her down. Jules had enough passion to satisfy the hunger of two women.

"In the sphere of love, those were our best years, Jules," she mused.

She rolled up the magazine and gave him a playful tap with it on his chest. It sounded hollow. She closed her eyes and concentrated on the heaving sensation in her abdomen. Wasn't it strange that her love for him had flared up just when he'd been about to leave her? Now that he really had left her, tenderness flared up. A feeling of connection that didn't oppress her.

"I am going to miss you, Jules," she said. "Everything will be different. And yet I find it easier to surrender you to death than to life. I'd rather see you disappear from my life holding the hand of a translucent angel than that of a woman of flesh and blood."

If he could, he would have laughed at her now. An angel! Female romanticism! Jules believed in the Grim Reaper, cloaked in a black priest's robe, the executioner's hood low over his brow. But try as she might, Alice couldn't imagine that the Man with the Scythe was sitting there, with a grin on his rock-hard head, beside her husband on the sofa. Jules's body might well be petrified and chilled, but he looked more vulnerable than she had ever seen him look when he was alive and well. She had no difficulty, on the other hand, picturing an angel beside him, with supple feathered wings and a face that could be a man's as well as a woman's.

"Anyway, Jules," she said, suddenly anxious to wrap up the subject once and for all. "Your holiday with Olga never took place, and that was my doing. A business trip, a conference … what a transparent excuse. I had really expected a little more originality from a man like you. Bank clerks don't go to conferences in London, not even if they work for an English bank. At most, they get a further training course from ten to four, with sandwiches for lunch and a drink afterwards. In the company cafeteria. I only had to call your boss to find out that you were lying. He never breathed a word about it to you. But he never forgot — I could tell from his knowing look at the reception for your twenty years of service. I remember exactly what he said. A tower of strength, a man of his word ... then he turned his eyes away from you and gave me a quick glance. I called Olga too, at work. At least, that was my intention. I was only too aware that I might be signing my own death warrant. If I admitted openly that I knew, what would prevent the two of you from going away together? To start a new life together? But luck was on my side. When I asked for Mrs. Javurkova in the import department, the switchboard operator said: 'Do you mean Mrs. Van den Eerenbeemt?' So that was her husband's name, apparently.

"I put the receiver down at once. According to the telephone book, only one Van den Eerenbeemt lived in the backwater where Olga's small farmhouse was located. The rest was child's play. I called him and said I was the wife of the man his Olga was having an affair with. And I told him that very soon she would spin him a yarn about a business trip." She watched for a reaction on Jules's face, as if she expected him to explode with fury. Or burst out laughing perhaps, after all these years. Had his eyelids begun to droop, was his gaze more inward than this morning?

"The next day, you came home with the news that your conference had been cancelled. For weeks you were in a terrible mood, Jules, but I put up with this because I knew it was over between you and Olga. You turned away from me. You gnashed your teeth in your sleep. You even cuffed Herman's ears for a triviality once. It is the only time you have ever hit your son, and he was already almost grown-up. I calmed him down. Sitting on the foot of his bed, in which he lay sobbing with indignation, I said that he should forgive you. That you were having a rough time and weren't quite yourself. It gradually sank in that his father was only human. Men, too, are allowed to cry, I told Herman. And if they can't, they are allowed to slap occasionally."

Her mouth was dry. But before she went to the kitchen to make tea, she wrapped her arms around Jules and kissed him on his ice-cold lips.

"Please don't be angry with me," she said. "I'm so glad I finally came out with it."

She warmed her hands around the big mug of tea. "Mom," was written in red letters on the white earthenware. The one with "Dad" would remain in the cupboard for good. It was a hideous but well-meant Christmas present from Herman in his teenage years, cherished year after year and still unbroken. Alice always felt a bit ridiculous when they drank from them. Yet they did so now and then, as a mark of honour to their only son.

She sat down across from Jules. The tabletop felt cool, right through her woollen skirt. But it was a different kind of coolness than that of the white aura now surrounding Jules's form. He was an immovable iceberg, a frozen fire with a cape of snow around his shoulders. Alice sniffed the air, her head tilted back. Did she smell something? Or was it fear of witnessing the impermanence of his familiar body? The heavy odour of a slept-in, rumpled bed and the well-known body smells rising from the laundry basket drifted into her nostrils. She wasn't sure whether it was a memory, a craving for life, or a reality.

She must do something. But the thought of strangers breaking up the intimacy with their arrangements was unbearable to her. They would soothe and comfort her, perhaps give her a tranquillizer. While she felt so calm and peaceful. Her memory was in overdrive — images from the past unexpectedly popped into her mind like jacks-in-the-box. They would all tell her what to do, and she would no longer hear the gentle flow of her thoughts reaching Jules. Just a little while longer, she vowed to herself, just a little while longer.

She set herself a deadline. Early in the evening I'll call Herman. Then he will have arrived home from work, Aimée can take care of him and drive him over here. A man shouldn't be told in the middle of a meeting that his father has died, and a man shouldn't drive a car when he has just heard that he is no longer a child with two parents.

Outside, dusk was falling. Alice would have liked to stop time. To freeze in the moment with Jules. To extinguish daylight with Jules.

The Mom mug had cooled off in her hands. She could have sworn Jules's beard had grown. A dark shadow had stolen over his chin, throat, and temples. Death had erased his age. He looked like her father in his younger days, and out of the image of her father emerged the figure of their son. As he sat there, present and gone at the same time, he embodied all the loved and hated men in her life. Alice sat perfectly still until darkness had descended completely.

She drifted in the twilight zone between waking and sleeping. Time went its own way. Until an impulse prompted her to get up, pick up the telephone, and call her son. But in that one moment of hesitation, while she massaged her stiff knees, she got talking to Jules again. And the moment passed.

"I so dread calling Herman, Jules," she said.

She walked through the room, switched on the lamps. She saw the streetlights flashing on outside. The light infused new life into their togetherness.

"I know how it is. He has just arrived home from work, he is tired, perhaps he is having a drink with Aimée or they are busy cooking together. And then I come and spoil everything with my announcement. Their cooking together, by the way, has always made me envious of them. You have stuck to your principles right up to yesterday: cooking is women's work. That you began making coffee in the morning after your retirement was already quite an accomplishment."

Normally, she cloaked her criticisms in careful banter. But today the last word was undeniably hers.

"I would find it much easier to say to a daughter that her father is dead than to a son," she mused. "Women are better able to cope with such things. I know already that in the days to come I'll be more worried about Herman than about myself. A daughter … If, that time in Paris, it was a daughter, she would be fifty-two now. Just imagine, Jules, a middle-aged woman for a daughter. A woman with hot flashes and grey temples, rebellious because her waistline is disappearing and her breasts are beginning to sag …"

Her laugh shot out of her throat, made its way through the web of lines in her face. In her memory the lost daughter — if it hadn't been a son, that is — had always remained a little girl in a floral dress and tiny patent leather shoes. She had never developed crow's feet, never shed blood, never suffered pain. Once in a blue moon the child danced through Alice's memories like a merry ghost, especially when she heard Edith Piaf sing. She had sketched and coloured her unknown daughter according to her own vision, with a little doll from a Rie Cramer book as a model.

She had only seen the never-born child for a couple of minutes. It was a blood clot in the bidet of a Paris hotel room. How privileged she had felt to be able to spend a whole honeymoon week in the City of Light. For the first time in her life she found herself abroad.

Jules was sent out by his bank every so often to sort things out at a branch office in Paris. Two weeks after their marriage, they had been able to combine business with pleasure and had gathered honey from their *lune de miel*.

Alice's head had spun from all the worldly impressions: shops, restaurants, elegant waiters, clochards, the Eiffel Tower. Inside, within the four walls of their cheap hotel room, she had learnt about love. The subtleties, because, contrary to the customs and traditions of the time, they had experimented with the basics at home. Alice couldn't say as she'd cared much, though, for the stolen Sunday afternoons in her girl's bed. Her heart was in her mouth, and her blush spread far beneath the sheets, from pure fear that her parents might come home earlier than expected.

In Paris it was different. She felt free, she let herself go completely in the hard hotel bed that panted and squeaked rhythmically under their bodies as if it were making love itself. She found it exciting to hear people walking right past their door. Snatches of French conversation, thumping, giggling — the background noises and those of the bed fused into a cheerful sound-and-light show.

On the night before they left they were to go to a musical. The opening act was to feature a young, as yet unknown singer: Edith Piaf.

"You looked smart, Jules. You had brilliantine in your hair and wore a snow white shirt. I remember vividly how you smelled when I helped you with the stud of your detachable collar, my nose grazing your neck. Like a man who didn't have to wait anymore, who no longer needed to be careful like a boy. I wore an evening gown of blue moiré, borrowed from my aunt. Because in my own wardrobe a white blouse with a piqué collarette was the most festive piece and, of course, that was too dull for the Parisian nightlife. Remember?"

Alice could effortlessly conjure up the feel of the fabric. It was the tight-fitting skin of a fish, but in a warm version. Dark and light shadows folded around her body's every movement.

"Already in the afternoon, I began to feel sick," she said in a small voice. "I had a stomach ache. I suspected that all that *faire l'amour* was taking its toll. Or was my period, the first as a married woman, announcing itself? It would be the first time I'd have to fuss with rags and cramps in front of you. I suddenly got terribly cold but stepped out of my dress all the same so as not to crease it. I lay down on the bed for a moment, and right away there was that warm moistness, along with a single stab of pain. Blood and the thrust of a knife. We ended up having to pay for the stained bedspread — that upset our plans. I should have asked you to put it in the washbasin in cold water. You helped me onto the bidet, Jules, and I felt ashamed to be sitting there so nakedly, while something slippery slid out of my body. When the doctor arrived, called by the hotel's receptionist, it still lay bright red on the bidet's white porcelain, like a tiny chicken liver.

"A miscarriage at a very early stage, the doctor said with an expert's eye. That I had been pregnant, even got married while pregnant, didn't register with me until much later. At first, I worried about the soiled bedspread and about the bloody little pile that wouldn't go down the drain. You picked it up with a newspaper and threw it in the *poubelle*. Our first child was buried in *Le Soir Illustré*. We covered it up with our conspiracy — no one has ever known. We never had to lie about a premature firstborn. But between the two of us we never talked about it again either, and I wonder if the image of a little curly-haired princess or a tiny soccer player with scraped knees has once in a while flashed past your eyes, too."

Alice would never know.

"This secret, which you are taking to your grave, is one we share, at least," she said. "A better secret, too, than that of Olga. Although both took place in a hotel room with a local doctor in a supporting role."

She needed to think about that for a moment, about secrets in hotel rooms. It had to be a coincidence. She pulled a drawer of the wall cabinet open and slid her finger over the row of cassettes. "*Je ne regrette rien*," etc., *Edith Piaf*, was written in Jules's hand.

They hadn't gone to the nightclub that evening. They hadn't heard the young Edith Piaf. At the recommendation of the doctor, Alice had remained flat on her back for one night, with Jules snuggling against her. She remembered his hand, never moving, on her empty belly. Through his motionless fingertips, the realization had slowly trickled in: she had lost a child while she didn't even know it had nestled inside her. They hadn't spoken to each other that night, hadn't exchanged a single word.

When, the following morning, the small plastic waste-paper basket was emptied and their cardboard suitcase stood ready, the forgetting had already begun.

She would put on some music, cuddle up against Jules. Although she knew better, she tried to detach his hand from his knee. What she wouldn't have given to be able to feel his warmth one more time in the place where for all those years she had cherished the memory of their Parisian child. But his hand was cold and unyielding. No longer capable of caressing.

She must call Herman. Now. She couldn't put it off anymore.

Then the telephone rang. The unexpected sound went right through her. She let it ring four times. As she reached for the receiver, she planted her feet firmly on the ground. She heard breathing, deep and hurried, even before the voice entered her ear.

"Mrs. Alice," Bea said, "I'll come straight out with it. My mother isn't doing well. It all turned out to be much worse than they initially thought. Internal bruising, complications ..."

The torrent of words stopped briefly. There was the muffled sound of Bea blowing her nose. Alice very nearly took advantage of the pause to hang up. She had her own inner bruising to contend with. But Bea got a hold of herself and carried on.

"Mrs. Alice, you know I would never impose on your hospitality, especially now that Mr. Jules isn't well. But I really don't know what to do with David. And I must go and visit my mother. I must! Suppose things go wrong without my having seen her again. But I don't dare take David along. Of course, I can leave him in the hallway of the hospital and ask him to wait. But he is so unpredictable, even more so in an unfamiliar building. Particularly in the evening. Besides, I want to spend a few quiet, undisturbed moments alone with my mother …"

Bea now cried openly. Alice hadn't actually heard her words. But the question hidden behind them had sunk in immediately. What should she say? That it wasn't convenient? Could she park David at the chessboard again? He wouldn't have told his mother anything, would he? No, that was impossible. His knowing look had reassured her more thoroughly than a signed contract could have done.

"Please, Mrs. Alice, may I bring David upstairs in a minute? You are the only person I can, and dare to, ask. With you and Mr. Jules, my son feels at ease. He was so relaxed this morning when he came down. I could call a babysitter, but then I wouldn't have a moment's peace. He doesn't tolerate any intruders in his territory …"

"Does he know his grandmother is doing poorly?" Alice heard herself ask, although she knew the reply wouldn't help her in any way.

"No, he doesn't," came the answer. "I need to let it sink in myself first. I'll let him know tomorrow. Not now, because he wouldn't sleep then. Perhaps after his chess game tomorrow. He is so attached to his fixed habits and patterns. To fixed people in his life, too. His grandmother, my mother ... I hope she'll pull through."

"Just put him in the elevator. We don't mind keeping him occupied for an hour or so," Alice said brusquely.

"I'll bring him up. I'll be there within ten minutes," Bea said in her usual take-charge voice again.

"All right, we're expecting him."

Alice replaced the receiver and straightened up. A strange calm descended on her. She strode to the kitchen, saw on the clock that it was already after half past six.

"I forgot to eat. I even forgot to feel hungry," she said half to herself, half to Jules's profile. "Perhaps I can have a sandwich with David." In her mind she took stock of the contents of the refrigerator.

"I'm leaving you alone for a minute, Jules. We'll just have to see what happens."

She walked back to the hallway, carefully closed the door to the living room and stationed herself by the front door. She squinted through the peephole at the tiled no man's land, to which she had tried without success to add a homey touch with a small Persian carpet. She laid her ear on the smooth wood of the door and gathered, from what she heard as well as sensed, that the elevator was on its way. Bea wore a long black winter coat. Her hair was tucked away under a black beret. Between the two dark surfaces hung a crimson scarf.

"They are here, Jules," Alice called out over her shoulder on a whim.

"I am eternally grateful to you," Bea said. With her hand, she nudged her son towards the door opening.

"Oh, that's much longer than necessary," Alice quipped in reply.

"Is Mr. Jules all right?" Bea asked.

Her mouth was a hand's breadth above David's dark hair. Alice noticed how tall he had already grown. Or did Bea happen to be small for a mother?

"Is Mr. Jules all right?" she repeated when no answer was forthcoming. The top layer of David's hair stirred, lifted by her breath.

"He's holding his own," Alice said. "The same as this morning."

Then she saw a change come over David's face. It was a nearly imperceptible quiver just under the skin. The knowing look sparked in his eyes again, a secret sign between conspirators.

"Come on in, my boy," she said. She had to restrain herself from resting her hand on his shoulder.

"I'll call you as soon as I can."

Bea's voice was smothered by the peck she gave on David's cheek. He shook off the imprint of her lips as if it were a fly.

"Good luck with your mother," Alice said while watching Bea disappear into the elevator. But it was only when David stood in the little hallway and she double locked the door that she could truly relax.

She looked at him hesitantly. What should she do with him? How was she going to keep him amused? For hours, perhaps. She could turn on the television. But it felt wrong to let the outside world intrude into the room where Jules was. To surround him with popular music, bluish light, the banality of a soap opera or a quiz show. It would be a trivialization of his death.

"How about starting a new chess game?" she asked David, who stood as motionless as a column directly under the hall light.

"But it isn't ten o'clock, Mrs. Alice."

It sounded almost scornful.

He clenched his hands into fists and pressed them against the sides of his jeans. Was he afraid, perhaps, she might force him to do something that didn't fit into his schedule?

"Come," Alice said. "We are going to sit by Mr. Jules. And then you can tell me in a little while what you would like to do, all right? Read a book perhaps? Or play a card game? We could also get a jigsaw puzzle out of the cupboard. I have them up to two thousand pieces."

She opened the living-room door and the stuffy smell hit her in the face. She shivered. Something had to be done soon. In the bathroom, she snatched up Jules's bottle of aftershave and tucked it into the pocket of her cardigan.

David followed her like a little dog, adjusting his steps to hers. He stood watching Jules's petrified body for a long time, but his face didn't show even a hint of fear.

"Mr. Jules is dead," Alice said softly.

She wanted to remind the boy. And herself.

David stole closer, briefly made a flitting movement with his right hand. When he had himself under control again, he slowly trailed his fingers over the marble face. He traced tender tracks on the forehead and the cheeks, like an exorcism.

"Mr. Jules is gone. This is the outside of Mr. Jules," he said.

Alice cried again. She thanked her lucky stars that there was no grey undertaker sitting in her living room who would give a polite cough and wait until she had collected herself again. That she didn't need to hide her own sadness to soothe the grief of her son. That the family doctor didn't quietly give her a sleeping pill as balm for a wound that really wasn't one. She counted her blessings on this white day. Jules had deflated like a balloon. Life had completely drained out of him. The umbilical cord that joined his old, cumbersome body with hers and with life had grown increasingly thin and frayed. Now it had broken. Jules had flowed into her as the day wore on. She had stored in the deepest recesses of her inner self all that shouldn't be forgotten, all that had united them in good days and bad.

The petrified body sitting there on the sofa was the outside of Mr. Jules. It was his worldly coat, which he'd stepped out of.

"The outside of Mr. Jules," David repeated. A broad smile landed on his ever-serious face.

He understood perfectly. A lifeless man on a sofa and an old woman who treated this as an accomplished fact were within his comprehension. They radiated certainty and security. Jules would definitely remain sitting in his spot, his hands fused with his knees, his half-closed eyes fixed on nothing, surprise scored like a line between his nose and chin. She herself wouldn't move more than a few metres out of David's field of vision as long as he was here. No unexpected things would happen in this room where everything had its place as in a chess game. That reassured David. And, therefore, her as well.

It was a moment of insight, of wordless joy for Alice. She felt the hunger gnawing at her stomach.

"Have you had your supper, David?" she asked.

The everyday question briefly unnerved him. He breathed quickly and audibly, spread his arms and fingers as though he wanted to take off. For a moment, he was an eagle, ready for flight. Then he folded his wings again.

Alice could almost hear the rustling of the feathers. He hid his hands under his armpits, as if to keep himself from making a second attempt.

"No," David said. "Mom didn't give me anything to eat tonight. She was scared."

"Then you and I are going to have something to eat. Because I'm hungry too, now that I'm no longer scared," Alice replied.

He smiled. His arms dropped limply beside his lanky body. Alice made up her mind not to ask him any more questions. Not about food. And not about fears. She needed to present him with accomplished facts.

"Messy, messy, messy," he sang when he stepped into the tiny kitchen. This was the first time he spontaneously made a remark, without her having spoken to him beforehand.

She had to agree with him. The coffee maker, brought to life by Jules shortly before he breathed his last, stood in the middle of the counter, with some leftover coffee in the glass carafe. She hadn't taken away Jules's plate, which was untouched. The jar of jam and the jar of mayonnaise were open. Traces of butter stuck to the knife. The crumpled ball of shrimp paper gave off a stale smell that mixed with that of the cold coffee.

"If Mr. Jules saw this, he would have a heart attack," Alice said as she began to tidy up. She laughed at her own joke, and noticed it had a contagious effect on David. When he felt ill at ease, he grew rigid like a robot. But security was translated by his body into loose-hanging arms, limp as those of a rag doll. And into a smile that conjured up Marcellino *pane e vino* again.

"I'm going to cook a delicious little meal for us," she announced. "I'll just see what I've got on hand."

The prospect sent a surge of energy through her body. She saw how David pulled the doors of the tall corner cupboard open. She was on the verge of calling him to order. But when she saw his eyes wandering over the well-stocked shelves, she realized that at his own place, three floors down, he probably had the same sort of cupboard in the same corner. He asked no questions, picked a yellowish orange box from the assortment and held it out to Alice.

"Instant pancake mix," she read. In case a war should break out all of a sudden, Jules used to say about such concessions.

"Do you feel like pancakes?" she asked.

David wasn't listening. With his back straight as an arrow, he bent his knees, stuck his head halfway into the cupboard under the sink, and took out a frying pan. Next, he opened the refrigerator and, with the greatest care, laid out beside the gas stove a bottle of milk, a partially used package of butter, and two eggs, which, in her confusion, she had apparently overlooked this morning. She sat down on one of the kitchen chairs, saw David's eyes travel over cupboards and shelves. She tried to think of what item might still be missing. Brown sugar? A whisk? An apple and cinnamon perhaps? She herself always added a dash of soda water to the batter, for lightness.

David lifted the clivia plant, as old as her son and many times its original size, out of the white ornamental holder, gave it a quick sniff and slapped the pot down next to the eggs. A mixing bowl.

Years of conditioning prompted her to expect that Jules would walk in at this tense moment and ask her what she thought she was doing. If she had gone mad, letting a child carry on like this in her kitchen. Allowing it to beat eggs in a flowerpot. But he didn't walk in. He was there already. Inside her, like a child that had returned to its mother's womb. Her hand automatically went to her belly. She gave Jules a pat on the shoulder.

"I want two, one with brown sugar and one with honey," Alice said to David.

"So do I. And an apron," he commanded.

While Alice tied her striped apron at his back, he broke the first egg on the rim of the pot with the deftness of a professional cook. His body heat rose against her own chilled limbs. She sat down again. Waited and sniffed, longing for the sugary smell to settle in every corner of the kitchen. Was it possible that she felt completely balanced? While Jules sat, dead, in the living room and David silently made pancakes in her kitchen? It was possible. She knew it for certain, in that one lucid moment before she began to nod. They were attuned to each other. All three of them did exactly what needed to be done, considering the circumstances. Wind and weather permitting.

Alice, wading through blue fumes, set the table for the two of them. She slid Jules's breakfast plate over to her own spot. She even folded napkins and lit a candle. The tiny space was choked with baking smells. They trailed into the living room and wrapped Mr. Jules's form in a sweet haze.

The pancakes were just as they should be: brown spotted on the outside, soft on the inside. Alice sprinkled hers with a crackling layer of brown sugar, rolled them up, and cut off parallel slices. Her upbringing lasted a lifetime. With mathematical precision David cut squares and triangles from his. At every bite, his gaze turned inward and his long lashes briefly winged up and down. The temptation lurked to strike up a normal conversation with him. Where he had learnt to make such perfect pancakes. If perhaps he wanted to become a cook later on. Where his father was. If he realized just what situation he found himself in.

She asked none of the questions that bubbled up in her. She had understood David's directions for use: he could only do one thing at a time. And he did this with so much dedication that the outside world fell away.

Alice ate. In silence. Every now and then she gave the boy an encouraging nod. But her smile glanced off his face, which was of impenetrable marble, like Jules's. David's chewing jaws, the only part that moved in his stiff, brooding face, reminded her of the living Jules. With him, the grim grinding of his jaw had heralded the first signs of rage.

She couldn't quite finish her pancake and left the last two centimetres on her plate, along with her knife and fork, placed side by side, and spread out her napkin on top. David opened his eyes ominously wide. She instinctively reached for her napkin, dabbed her lips as if she'd taken a little break, and finished her plate like an obedient child. With her finger she vacuumed up the last specks of brown sugar, and she very nearly licked her plate. Her skirt felt tight around her waist, her lips tasted greasy. She had eaten too much and would give anything for a nap, for half an hour of oblivion. What she really yearned for was to crawl into bed, with the soft flannel fabric of her nightgown around her legs, and slip away into the no man's land of sleep. Not for a moment did she think about the empty place. In her mind, Jules was still the familiar wall of warmth behind her back.

"Shall we just leave everything?" she suggested. She was tired. But David was already busy gathering the plates and cutlery and stacking everything on the left-hand side of the counter. Before she knew what was happening, his arms were in suds up to his elbows. She grabbed a tea towel and took up a waiting position to his right. "You eat together, you do the dishes together," her mother used to say. But David thought differently.

"The outside of Mr. Jules is alone," he said.

The look in his eyes said: "Please leave the kitchen." She didn't need to be told twice. She meekly draped the checkered tea towel over the back of a chair and went to the living room.

"I'm exhausted, Jules," she said.

She no longer felt a need to tenderly stroke his hair or plant a kiss on his granite cheek. Could a dead person shrink? His skin seemed too large. He looked ashen, and she even discovered shadows of bruises on his wrists. Or was that the reflection of the snow? She drew the curtains but the bruises remained. She sat down beside him and laid her small blue-veined hands on his, which were large and broad, with square nails and blunt fingers. Hands like hams.

They were just like her father's hands, but Jules's hands had never hurt her. She had to say that much for him. Her father, though, had made her feel the iron grip of his fingers often enough. Spare the rod and spoil the child, was his motto. With all her might she suppressed memories of red-hot impressions of his hand on her cheek, of steel pliers around her thin arm. Immediately, a feeling of guilt surged up again, like the milk into her breasts long ago. Jules doesn't deserve that his hands lead me to my never-erased childish pain, she thought. And instantly, like a hamster scurrying out of its straw burrow, there was that one sweet memory hidden under the echo of slaps.

Alice sat on the luggage carrier of her father's bicycle. On a quiet, grey Sunday-morning street, they pedalled to the store to buy a present for Mother's Day, which had begun but not yet been celebrated. They chose a slender, crystal vase with azure edges along its flared top. The fragile object was first wrapped in tissue paper, then in gold-striped gift wrap, and finally, to be on the safe side, in the sports supplement of the Sunday newspaper. Perched behind his broad back, Alice held the trophy in front of her chest like a standard-bearer holding his furled flag. And then her father cycled into a hole in the road and they lay together on the paving stones. Miracle of miracles, the vase was intact, but when the bicycle capsized, her right foot got stuck between the gyrating spokes. Above her sandal, her skin had turned into a tiny pleated skirt with blood pooling underneath. She screamed, more with fear than pain. And then, from the solid suit of armour with hands like hams, emerged a gentle father. With utter calm he did what needed to be done, in the right order. First, he picked up the vase, still in its newspaper wrapping, and handed it to the barber who'd come to look what the clatter in front of his shop was about. He threw the bicycle against the wall, and, in the warm hollow encircled by his arms, carried his daughter inside. He set her down on the counter as if it were the table in their own house, and she saw her contorted face looking back at her from all the mirrors at once. A handkerchief with warm water, a handkerchief with cold water, a dab of spit — *daddy's ointment* he called it — and all was well again. Men with lathered faces, the hair on their heads slicked down like wet paintbrushes, followed the operation closely. They praised her for being so brave, and from the barber she got a toffee, which lasted all the way home. The best part of the memory was that on the trip back she was allowed to sit with her legs to one side on her father's bicycle's crossbar, which cut a furrow into her buttocks. In the safe space marked out by arms and legs, she breathed in time with him. The vase almost melted in her hands. And then, securely enclosed within her cage of human flesh, she noticed the violet bruises on her father's hands, the blackened blood on the scrape. There hadn't been a peep out of him while he smoothed out her pleated skin and dried her tears. Never in her life had she loved her father more unconditionally than at that moment. Or realized it, at least. The next time she was slapped, it hurt less.

Alice got up and went to the built-in cupboard in the kitchen, where she took the slender vase from the shelf. David was so engrossed in the drying of the cutlery that he didn't lift his eyes.

"Look," she said to Jules, "this was the one. Later, those bluish edges reminded me of a jellyfish. They still do, actually. But when we bought the vase, I had never seen a jellyfish. I remember that my mother was thrilled with it. She said it was an economical gift because it could only hold one or two flowers. After she died, I took it with me. I knew it represented something special, but I'd forgotten what. Now it is all rising to the surface again. Because of your blue hands."

She sat down in the leather armchair, the vase clasped between her hands. She heard the soft clatter in the kitchen at longer and longer intervals. She fell asleep like that. It wasn't a real, relaxed sleep, but the kind of dozing that often overcame her in the car. The mind took a short break, while thoughts were smothered under a woollen blanket, but the body felt every bump in the road.

With a start, she came back to reality. Had she actually been asleep, then? David had sat down beside Jules. His hands lay on his knees, his eyes were half-closed. He barely breathed. The sight moved her. In the space of a day, her husband's empty shell had become as familiar to her as his living, breathing body had been in all the preceding years. As the day progressed, the core of his being had flowed into her, and spread far and wide under her skin. He was part of her. No undertaker, no notary or priest could separate him from her anymore. Beside him sat the living boy, who adjusted himself to Jules's body like a shadow. Stock-still and completely at ease. Where, Alice thought, could he possibly feel better than here, in the no man's land between life and death, where the constellation of three people is fixed, the musty smell constant, and the sounds barely audible? Jules won't jump up suddenly, and I myself am no longer capable of anything but sitting and waiting. The only thing that can tear him away from this frozen tableau vivant is a phone call from his mother, which will eventually take him back to his own safe world. This reassured Alice. It freed her from banal thoughts about turning on the television or looking for something to do.

Time passed. Timelessly. Alice got up and peered through the crack between the curtains. It was snowing again. Lazily falling flakes blanketed the outside world with a thick layer of white. It made her head spin. She didn't see a single car light in the deserted street. Not a soul, nor a movement brought the world back from its hibernation. This was the perfect setting for a farewell, she realized. She couldn't bear to think that Jules might have departed on a glorious summer day, that she would sit here with him in air thick with barbecue smells and the exuberant hum of voices.

When she turned around, she saw that David's head had slumped backwards and his mouth was ajar. Every so often his lips twitched. He was asleep. She sat down again, rested her head against the back of the armchair. The image of her husband and the boy faded from her eyes. The darkness sucked her away in short naps. Until she surfaced in reality again and caught sight of the rigid body of the man beside the relaxed form of the boy. Again and again. And so the hours went by.

The shrill ringing of the telephone flung her ashore on a tall wave. Dazed, she looked around. David opened his eyes and instinctively threw up his arms like an actor in a play. Then he sunk back into the oblivion of sleep.

"You'd think the devil had a hand in it," Bea said at the other end of the line. "My mother is on the mend, fortunately. The danger has passed. It's only a question of time. But the problem is that I can't go home now. I got a terrible fright when I came out of the hospital. I could hardly find my car. There must be twenty centimetres of snow on it. To tell the truth, Mrs. Alice, I don't dare to drive. Even under normal conditions I'm a bit of a coward behind the wheel. How is David?"

"David?" Alice repeated to gain time. The torrent of words slowly slid into her mind, like a frozen river.

"We made pancakes together," she said.

"Oh yes, he's a whiz at that," his mother replied. "David is a wonderful cook. What is he doing now? I hope he isn't troublesome. He should have been in bed ages ago. Perhaps I ought to take a taxi, because I really don't dare to get into the car by myself. I could ask my brother if ... What do you think, Mrs. Alice, would there be any taxis running tonight?"

If there were any taxis running? That was the very last thing she was in the mood for.

"David is dozing on the sofa," Alice said. "You know what we'll do? I'll make up a bed for him. Then he doesn't have to wake up and you won't need to risk your life. As for tomorrow, we'll cross that bridge when we come to it. I'm sure you'll be able to spend the night at the hospital. Plenty of beds, I would think."

"But all that bother ... Do you have a spare bed?"

Her protest carried an undertone of relief.

"No, I don't have a real spare bed. But if I slip a pillow under his head and cover him with a blanket everything is solved."

This sounded so firm that she added more gently: "David and I get along well."

"And Mr. Jules? Won't he find it too inconvenient?"

"This is an emergency," Alice said.

Before Bea raised any more objections, Alice brought the conversation to an end.

"Just call me tomorrow morning when you get home," she said. "And if the worst comes to the worst, I can always go and put David in his own bed. Then I'll sit with him. I don't mind."

She no longer even heard Bea's reply. David was wide awake now. He sat huddled on the sofa, pale with sleepiness. His hands winged upwards like white butter-flies and landed restlessly on his knees.

"If I have to sleep on the sofa with a pillow and a blanket, where will the outside of Mr. Jules go?" he asked.

Fear loomed in his eyes while he estimated the distance between the body and the armrest. He flinched when Alice brushed past him. She sank back into her chair and stayed put, until he'd realized that she wasn't going to take action.

"I just said that to reassure your mom," she explained. "Don't worry, we'll find a good spot for you to sleep. You can also stay where you are on the sofa if you like, but then you're bound to become as stiff tonight as I am."

"Or as Mr. Jules." His voice sounded steady again.

"Of course not," Alice soothed. "Mr. Jules has died. He was an old man. His heart gave up. Yours is strong and healthy. It will go on beating for dozens of years."

His right hand fluttered up to his chest. By the trembling, Alice could see his heartbeat.

"You could also sleep in the big bed, now that there's an empty spot there tonight," Alice suggested hesitantly.

"Yes," David said, "I sometimes sleep in the big bed with Mom, too."

Without saying another word, he got up and headed directly for the bedroom. He examined the unmade bed, gave the floor and furniture a quick inspection as well, and began to straighten the duvet.

With the same determination as when he'd gathered his ingredients and utensils in the kitchen, he now walked around the bed to smooth out the last creases. The routine way in which he strode past the foot of the bed to close the curtains amazed her. Until she remembered that in his own apartment the daily patterns were enacted on the same floor plan.

"The snow stays outside, the warmth is inside," he said.

It sounded like a poem.

Alice switched on a table lamp and went to the bathroom. Should she lay out a towel for him? A clean pyjama top of Jules's perhaps? She hadn't had anyone staying overnight for years. She would ask him if there was anything else he needed. When she returned to the bedroom, he was lying in bed on his back in Jules's spot, his hands under his head. His pants and sweater lay neatly folded on the chair. He had kept on his pale blue T-shirt.

"It is nighttime. Now I go to sleep," David said, thereby adding a new stanza to his poem. He turned on his side, pulled the flowered duvet over his ears, and fell silent. Her "goodnight, my boy" received no response. She stood still by the bed for a little while longer. Then she could tell from the heaving of the flowery meadow that he had done what he said he would.

David's spot next to Jules was still warm. She stretched out her arm and, at the touch of the smooth marble, an unfathomable loneliness overcame her. She curled up against her husband's body like a child against its mother, seeking warmth and protection. But she came up against a wall of frightful cold, of unyielding resistance.

"Jules," she whispered. "Jules."

All the rest had been said. She planted a kiss on his temple, and the white chill continued to burn on her lips. She got undressed, slipped her nightgown over her body. In the bedroom, she heard David make a humming noise as he breathed. Not wanting to wake him, she didn't turn on the light. For a time, she sat on the side of the bed, staring at the drawn curtains, behind which, she knew, was the snow.

"The snow stays outside, the warmth is inside," she recited softly. Then she slid under the duvet, gingerly, holding her breath, so as not to wake the boy. Tears ran silently down her cheeks. Before long, the warm tunnel took her in and she, too, was asleep.

When she woke up and felt the empty spot beside her, she knew what she had to do. She lay there for a minute, basking in the smells of the warm bed, nestling behind her back like a shadow. When she smelled coffee, she got up. With stiff joints, her skin stretched too tight, she headed towards the aroma of a new day.

Of Related Interest

The Postman's Round
Denis Thériault, translated by Liedewy Hawke
978-1-55002-785-3
$19.99

This short, astonishing novel conjures up the solitary daily life of Bilodo, a postman who shares his Montreal apartment with his goldfish, Bill. As a result of his indiscretion (the steaming open of personal correspondence), Bilodo becomes involved in an exchange of haiku between the woman of his dreams, a Guadeloupean beauty, and Gaston Grandpré, an eccentric intellectual whose mail Bilodo delivers. Around these events, Denis Thériault weaves a passionate tragicomic love story full of twists and turns, but also rich in dazzling descriptions of lush, tropical landscapes and subtle evocations of the sober, precise art of the haiku.

The Milky Way
Louise Dupré, translated by Liedewy Hawke
978-1-55002-383-1
$21.99

Confident, hardworking, and practical, architect Anne Martin is living the good life in Montreal. Yet one day, high up in her apartment overlooking the city and the river, at the heart of her perfectly controlled universe, Anne witnesses a scene that causes a crack to appear in her life, a crack that slowly widens and eventually threatens her very existence.

At this time of lost certainty, Anne's work takes her to Tunis. There, among the ruins of Carthage, she meets Alessandro Moretti, an Italian archaeologist who is her senior by nearly twenty years and affects her as no one ever has. A struggle ensues, between love and jealousy, love and the fear of abandonment, love and other, even deeper fears.

Available at your favourite bookseller.

DUNDURN PRESS
www.dundurn.com

What did you think of this book?
Visit *www.dundurn.com*
for reviews, videos, updates, and more!